The Adventures of Whirtleberry

Michael Greig Forsyth

Balboa Press books may be ordered through booksellers or by contacting:

Balboa Press
A Division of Hay House
1663 Liberty Drive
Bloomington, IN 47403
www.balboapress.com
844-682-1282

ISBN: 978-1-9822-6935-7 (sc)
ISBN: 978-1-9822-6934-0 (e)

Print information available on the last page.

Balboa Press rev. date: 05/27/2021

BALBOA.PRESS
A DIVISION OF HAY HOUSE

The Adventures of Whirtleberry

This book is dedicated to Cherri, Cathleen, Kerry and Grace.

CHAPTER ONE

Whirtleberry and the Cold Morning

Whirtleberry is a little brown mouse who lives in a cosy little hole with a green door at the bottom of the garden. A hole that is right under an azalea bush. He lives there with his sister Flapjack.

One cold winter's morning Whirtleberry woke up and streeetched, shook his head and pulled up his little blanket right to the tip of his nose. Brrrr, it was so cold. His little nose twitched, and his little whiskers moved up and down and from side to side. He was hungry.

Whirtleberry jumped out of bed, put a scarf around his neck and crossed the frosty lawn towards the big house. He knew that he'd find some delicious food in the kitchen there.

His little hands and feet were so cold on the frosty lawn. He scurried along as fast as he could go. Every now and then he stopped and blew warm air onto his little feet and paws. Pfffhuh, Pffffuh! He rubbed his paws together and blew onto them some more. Pfffhuh, pffffhuh! It was so cold.

He scampered up the steps to the big house keeping an eye open for the cats and dogs that he knew would be around. The dogs were big and black and very jumpy and rough, but they liked the little mouse. BUT the cat had long sharp claws and long sharp teeth and the cat LOVED to eat little mice for breakfast.

At the top of the steps, he scurried across the veranda to a little hole in the corner of the door to the kitchen. It was a teeny, tiny hole just big enough for a teeny, tiny mouse to squeeze through.

He looked around the kitchen. It was so lovely and warm. There on the floor he found some seeds which he popped into his cheeks to keep them safe. Then, next to the stove he found a bit of bacon rind and he popped that into his cheeks. And there in a corner of the kitchen he saw a piece of cake that had dropped to the floor. He clapped his little paws together and picked it up. He didn't see the ginger cat on top of the counter which was watching him. He took the cake and scurried towards the hole in the corner of the door. As he got close to the door, he noticed the big cat racing towards him. A big ginger cat with sharp teeth and long, shiny claws. The cat was licking its lips and clashing its teeth together. It was very frightening.

Whirtleberry raced closer and closer to the hole, the cat was right behind him. He squeeezed his fat little body through the hole which was much too small for the cat to fit through, and he raced across the veranda and down the steps, carefully holding the piece of cake between his paws.

He dashed across the cold frosty lawn and back to his little burrow under the azalea bush. When he got inside his sister, Flapjack, was just waking up. She squeaked with excitement when she saw Whirtleberry and the food. Flapjack pulled on her warm, sheepskin slippers and put on her pink winter dressing gown and they both sat down at their tiny table for breakfast.

CHAPTER 2
Whirtleberry at the Stream

Whirtleberry and Flapjack were so excited. They had overheard the humans in the big house talking about going for a picnic at the stream. They had been to the stream once before and it had been such fun.

The two little mice put on their swimming costumes, slung their tiny little striped towels over their shoulders and some sunglasses over their eyes. They thought that they looked really smart.

They listened carefully to the humans and as soon as they saw them starting to pack the little blue truck they scampered across the lawn and they snuck onto the truck and made themselves comfortable in a little hole in the back of the truck.

The two big, black dogs, Buddy and Callie jumped in too. They sniffed at where Whirtleberry and Flapjack were hiding and then, not being interested in little mice they stuck their heads out of the window and barked happily at the thought of a ride.

The little blue truck started up and the dogs barked with happiness. Whirtleberry and Flapjack hugged one another with excitement as the truck bounced down the road and they started their adventure to the stream.

After a little while they felt the little blue truck slowing down and then stopping. The dogs jumped off the back and rushed around in circles, sniffing at everything and then they ran to the cool water of the stream. The humans got out some deck chairs, a picnic blanket and, most importantly, a picnic basket. Delicious smells came from the picnic basket.

Whirtleberry and Flapjack hopped off the truck and found a nice patch of shade close to the picnic basket. They put their little striped towels down and set off towards the stream.

It was so exciting at the stream. They peered in and saw some crabs with their big claws, walking sideways on the stream-bed. In one of the pools were dozens of tadpoles wiggling their tails and swimming around. Nearby was a rock shaped just like a canoe and they scrambled onto it.

At that moment Buddy jumped into the water and a great wave of water splashed across the rock and washed Whirtleberry and Flapjack into the water. What could they do? The water was flowing fast. They squeaked and held onto one another as they got tumbled around in the water. Water splashed over them and they choked and spluttered.

Just then one of the humans stepped into the water and said, "Oh look at these little mice. They are getting swept away!" The human reached down and picked them up and put them onto the bank. They scampered back to their little towels and dried themselves then crept towards the picnic blanket and settled down on the edge.

There was delicious food to eat. Bacon and egg sandwiches, cheese, rolls, and some delicious sticky cake.

The humans didn't seem to mind them being there and they broke off bits of sandwiches and cake for the little mice to eat.

After lunch Whirtleberry and Flapjack stretched out in the sun and had a lovely nap. Then they packed their things, squeezed onto the little blue truck and, the dogs panting and drooling next to them, they rode home.

They'd had an exciting day out.

CHAPTER 3

Whirtleberry picking
MULBERRIES

Whirtleberry woke up and streeeeched! It was a lovely Spring day. The sun was shining, and the trees looked so pretty with their green leaves.

Whirtleberry gave his sister, Flapjack, a little nudge with his elbow and she opened her eyes wide. "Good morning" she said and rubbed her little sniffly, whiffly nose against his. Their whiskers went up and down, up and down and from side to side as fast as can be.

They had a little breakfast of some pieces of fruit that Whirtleberry had found next to the bird table and had brought home. After breakfast they went to the little door of their burrow and opened it wide. "What shall we do today Whirtleberry?" said Flapjack.

Whirtleberry looked around and thought hard. Then he saw the mulberry tree at the gate. It was covered with delicious looking fruit. His mouth watered at the thought of popping a plump berry into his mouth. "I know Flapjack, let's go and pick some mulberries."

They took a little basket and scampered across the lawn to the mulberry tree. Some of the branches stretched down low to the grass so Whirtleberry and Flapjack could easily scramble up these branches, but they wanted to get higher up the tree where the biggest, plumpest, juiciest mulberries could be found.

There was a sudden flapping and a squawk and a large Toppie bird landed on the branch next to them. It gave Whirtleberry and Flapjack quite a fright, but they soon saw that it was friendly. The Toppie told them that the very best mulberries could be found at the tippy top of the tree. "It's too high for us to get there", said Whirtleberry. "Don't worry, I'll help you said Mr Toppie. "Climb onto my back and I'll fly you to the top branches."

Whirtleberry and Flapjack scrambled onto Mr Toppie's back who took off and first of all flew high into the sky so that the two little mice could look down on the garden from far above. Then the kind Mr Toppie flew to the top branch of the mulberry tree and Whirtleberry and Flapjack jumped off his back and onto the topmost branch. "Call me when you want to get down and I'll come and fetch you," said Mr Toppie.

Whirtleberry found the biggest, juiciest mulberry and popped it into his mouth. Juice streamed down his chin. Oh, it was so delicious. Soon he and Flapjack were eating mulberries as fast as they could. The dark, sticky juice was everywhere. They looked at one another and burst out laughing. Their faces and whiskers and little paws were stained purple with all of the mulberry juice. They quickly filled their basket and called out to Mr Toppie to come and fetch them.

Mr Toppie flew down and perched on the branch and Whirtleberry and Flapjack climbed onto his back and he quickly flew down to the lawn outside their little burrow and dropped them off.

"Thank you Mr Toppie", said the little mice, "We are going to make some mulberry jam now and we will invite you to tea soon for delicious hot scones with cream and mulberry jam."

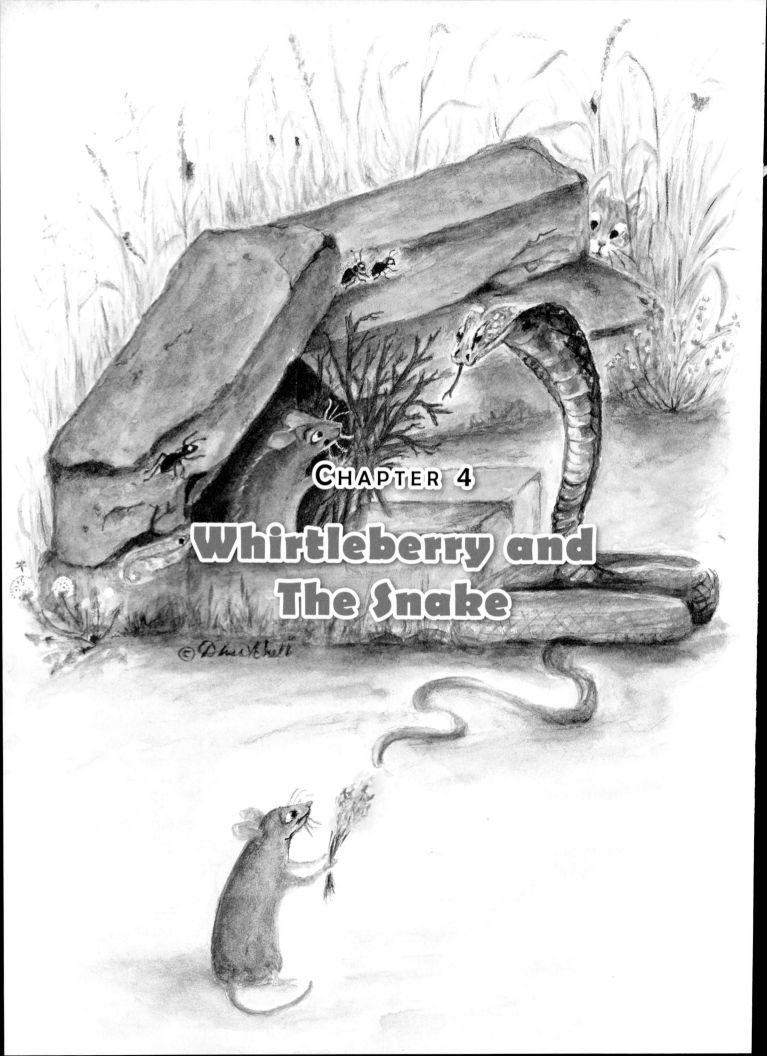

CHAPTER 4

Whirtleberry and
The Snake

It was a hot day. The sun was shining brightly when Whirtleberry started to walk around the garden to see what he could find to eat. There were lots of seeds and nuts and bits of bread and cake that the humans had dropped when they had picnicked in the garden the day before. Whirtleberry was happy.

Whirtleberry scampered around a big pile of bricks that were in the corner of the garden to see what was on the other side. He froze when he saw a great big snake slithering across the vegetable garden towards the pile of bricks just where he was.

The snake's tongue flicked in and out, in and out and its cold, beady eyes looked from side to side. What could Whirtleberry do? Where could he hide?

He spotted a hole in the bricks and started to move towards the hole. As he moved the snake caught sight of him and with a great HISSSS it shot forward towards him.

Whirtleberry squeeeezed into the hole in the pile of bricks and went down the hole as far as he could go. He so hoped that the hole was too small for the snake to follow him. His little heart beat pitty pat, pitty pat and his little whiskers twitched up and down, up and down and from side to side.

He turned around so that he could see down the hole towards the entrance. He saw the cold eye of the snake looking down the hole and its tongue flicking in and out. The snake hissed, "I'm coming to EAT YOU UP." Whirtleberry closed his eyes and shouted as loudly as he could for his sister, Flapjack, to come to help him.

Whirtleberry looked around the hole between the bricks and found a whole lot of twigs and sticks that he pushed firmly across the hole. He hoped that this would stop the snake from getting any closer.

The hole seemed to get darker as the snake slowly slithered down the passage towards Whirtleberry. The little mouse shivered and shook at its approach. He hoped that his sticks and twigs would give him a bit of time. He closed his eyes and yelled to Flapjack again.

To his great joy he heard Flapjack calling back. "I'm coming Whirtleberry" she shouted. "How big is the snake?" "It's HUGE," he said.

The snake came right up to the criss-cross twigs. It put it's lips right against the twigs and said: "I'm going to swallow you up". Its tongue flicked an and out again and its head started to press against the twigs. Whirtleberry could hear the twigs start to crack. His little heart was beating so fast it felt like it was coming out of his chest.

The snake pushed harder and harder but the next moment it said "OUCH!" and started to back up down the tunnel. "Ouch, ouch, ouch!" it said. And got further and further away from Whirtleberry.

What do you think had happened? Brave little Flapjack had found some very dry twigs and some matches and had set the twigs on fire. Then she bit SO HARD on the snake's tail, and when the snake popped out of the hole, she rushed at it with the burning twigs. The snake was so afraid of the fire that it turned around and slithered away as fast as it could.

Whirtleberry came scampering out of the hole and hugged and hugged and HUGGED Flapjack. He was so proud of his brave little sister.

They went back to their burrow and had their breakfast: a delicious cup of rose hip tea and a piece of cake.

CHAPTER 5
Whirtleberry and the swimming pool

The sun was shining as Whirtleberry and Flapjack put on their swimming costumes, slung their little striped towels over their shoulders, placed their sunglasses over their noses and off they set for the swimming pool.

Flapjack carried a teeny, tiny picnic basket with her. Inside were some little cucumber sandwiches, some muffins, and some juice to drink.

They got to the pool. It was their first swim for the summer, and they had forgotten how HUGE the pool was. It was a sparkly blue. Little waves lapped across the surface.

Kersplash! Kersplash! Buddy and Callie, the big black dogs, jumped into the pool. They splashed water all around and stood on the pool steps noisily lapping water. Callie blew bubbles under the water with her nose. Bbbbbbbbbb! She sneezed and looked around. Then both she and Buddy jumped out of the pool and shook themselves. Water showered around them, and big drops fell onto Whirtleberry and Flapjack. It felt like being out in the rain. The water droplets were so lovely and cool on such a hot day.

Aaah, it was time for a swim. Whirtleberry and Flapjack dived off the side of the pool. They both had little tubes to keep them afloat. Oh, it was such fun to go Splash, Splash in the Water. They bobbed around and swam little races. They closed their eyes and played Marco Polo. Round and around they swam, ducking their head under water and blowing bubble just like Callie. They laughed at the rude noise it made. Thbbbb!

After a while they started getting tired and wanted to get out of the pool. They swam towards the steps and then "Oh my goodness!" the steps were too high for them to get out of the pool. They both scrabbled at the steps, but the water was too low. Oh, how they started to squeak and squeak. They were so scared. What were they going to do?

Their squeaks made Big Black Buddy look up. He pricked up his ears and looked into the pool where he saw Whirtleberry and Flapjack splashing and scrabbling. He jumped into the pool and swam out a bit then swam back towards the steps. He had thick black fur and Whirtleberry and Flapjack were able to grab onto his fur and puuuuull themselves onto his back. Buddy swam once around the pool and then clambered out. He shook his fur to dry it and Whirtleberry and Flapjack flew off his back and landed head-over-heels on the soft lawn with a gentle bump.

They were so happy to have made it out of the pool. They ran around the lawn and Buddy and Callie ran next to them, quite happily. They all laughed and laughed remembering their adventure. Then they all lay down in the shade of a tree and fell fast asleep.

CHAPTER 6

Whirtleberry and the beehive

Bzzzzzz, bzzzzzzzz, bzzzzzzz! There were big yellow bees buzzing around the azalea bush. Bees with yellow coats and black stripes and great big stings sticking out of their bottoms.

Whirtleberry and Flapjack watched the bees. Their heads turned round and round as they watched them. It was a lovely spring day, and the bees were collecting pollen and nectar from the flowers in the garden.

Whirtleberry LOVED the honey that the bees made in their hive. The great combs of golden honey that dripped out and was so, so sweet. Whirtleberry's mouth started to water at the thought of eating some of the honey. But how was he to get any? He didn't want to get stung.

Whirtleberry thought hard about what to do. Think, think...Then he HAD it. He would disguise himself as a bee. He shouted to Flapjack to come to him and he told her of his BIG PLAN!

He asked her to help him look through the dress-up clothes they had from when they were at school. There in the dress-up chest were two bee outfits. Big yellow coats with black stripes and great big stings sticking out of the bottom. Just like the bees.

Squeaking with excitement Whirtleberry and Flapjack squeezed into their bee outfits. Whirtleberry put some goggles over his eyes so that the bees wouldn't sting them. Then they went to the garage and found a long piece of string, a basket and some gloves. I wonder what all of these things were for?

The little mice went out to the garden to where the beehive stood under the shade of a big tree. They climbed up the broad trunk of the tree to where a branch grew out close to the beehive, Flapjack tied the rope around Whirtleberry's waist, tied the other end around her waist and slowly lowered Whirtleberry down towards the beehive.

Whirtleberry waved his arms in the air and made a buzzing noise. Bzzzz, Bzzz. Bzzz. He got closer and closer to the beehive. Some bees started flying around him and getting closer and closer. Whirtleberry was getting nervous as more and more bees swarmed around him. "Oh dear", he said to Flapjack, "I don't think that my bee outfit is much good. They seem to know that I'm not a bee. Please pull me up again."

Flapjack heaved at the rope and started pulling hard. The rope inched up but then it got snagged on a branch. She pulled harder and harder, but the rope wouldn't budge. Harder and harder she pulled until SNAP, the rope broke and Whirtleberry fell through the air and landed with a big CRASH right on the beehive. The beehive crashed to the ground and combs of honey went splattering across the lawn. Flapjack quickly climbed down the tree and ran to help Whirtleberry.

The bees were very angry and flew down to where Whirtleberry was lying on the ground. His bee costume was broken and his goggles had come off. The bees looked VERY angry as they flew around him. Flapjack grabbed Whirtleberry by the hand and pulled him along behind her. As they ran Whirtleberry scooped up a big piece of honeycomb and carried it with him, dripping honey all the way.

The bees were right behind them as they scampered towards their door. Luckily the door was open and they ran through it and slammed it shut behind them. They sat on the floor and laughed with relief. Then they gathered up the big, dripping honeycomb, made some tea and toast and sat back and talked some more about their adventure..

CHAPTER 7

Whirtleberry and the Songololo

It was a hot day in the summer. The Christmas singers were singing their loud high-pitched noise and Whirtleberry and Flapjack were taking a little walk around the garden. It was all so green and there were puddles in places because of the rain that had fallen. It was so interesting to see everything. The little mice went to one of the puddles to play. They put their little feet into the cool water and could feel the mud squidging between their toes. Whirtleberry gave Flapjack a little push and she fell into the puddle. She squeaked with indignation. Then she got a naughty little smile on her face. She scooped up a big ball of that squidgy, squelchy mud and suddenly stood up out of the puddle and smeared the mud all over Whirtleberry's face.

At first Whirtleberry was startled then he started to laugh. His little eyes peered through the mud, all sparkling and shiny. He raced into the puddle and grabbed some mud in his paws and smeared it all over Flapjack too. The edge of the pond was very slippery with mud and the little mice soon made a fine game of running towards the mud and throwing themselves down on their tummies and sliding across the mud and into the pool of water. It was such fun and soon they were covered in mud from head to toe.

They set off for the humans' swimming pool to get clean. On their way, as they walked through some moss and leaves, they heard a noise. It was something saying in a squeaky voice, "One, two three four, five, six...oh dear I can't count more than that." The mice looked around, and there behind a tree, they saw a strange looking creature. It was as long as a bean and a dark brown colour. It had feelers on its head and so many legs. It had hundreds of legs all moving along and making the creature look like a clockwork toy.

Whirtleberry and Flapjack moved towards the creature, which suddenly curled itself up into a tight circle, its many, many legs tucked tight underneath its body. They got closer and tapped it on its head, Suddenly, a squirt of smelly poop shot out with a thbbbbb noise. The little mice jumped back, shocked. This seemed very rude to them. They tapped it again, very cautiously and the creature slowly started to unwind. It kept its head tight inside and they heard a muffled voice saying, "What do you want?"

Whirtleberry stepped forward and put his head a bit closer to the creatures head and said, "Hello creature, we don't want to hurt you. We are two little mice called Whirtleberry and Flapjack and we just wanted to say hello and find out what you are. Please don't poop on us again."

"I'm a Songololo and I have lots and lots of legs. So many that I can't count them all. It gets very confusing sometimes. Can you help me to count them all?" He unrolled his body all the way and the mice could see teeny, tiny, twinkling eyes. He sat back and showed them all of the legs under his belly. The mice could not believe how many there were.

They started to count them: "One, two, three, four, five, six, seven, eight, nine, ten". Then Flapjack said, "Mr Songololo, why do you want to know how many legs you have? They all work. They can crawl and walk and run. That's really all you need to know isn't it?"

The Songololo put one foot on its cheek and thought hard. "You are right," he said, "I really don't need to know how many legs and feet I have. I am so lucky to have that many legs!"

Whirtleberry laughed and said "I have a little song about legs".

"One, two, three, four, all these legs and then some more

On and on they marching go, first the foot and then the toe.

Let's count them now the legs and feet, marching, marching down the street

Can you count them all with me? I can only count 'til three.

Some go slow and some go quick, here and there they give a kick

Let's try again to count below and help out Mr Songololo"

They all sang the song together and set off to go to the pool to get clean and then the little mice asked Mr Songololo home for tea.

CHAPTER 8

Whirtleberry gets
lost at the airport

Whirtleberry and Flapjack were so excited. Their humans were going to go to the airport to fly overseas and had told the little mice that they could come along on the journey as well.

Whirtleberry and Flapjack knew that they would have to pack warm clothes because they were going to go to a country with lots of snow. They looked through their cupboards and took out coats and beanies and little mittens and scarves and warm little boots to wear. Whirtleberry knew how cold his little paws could get in the frost at home so how cold would it be in the snow?

They had so much fun getting ready, and they looked at the back of their cupboard and found a big trunk with leather straps that had belonged to their grandmother. They folded their clothes so carefully and filled up the trunk. They squeezed little bits and pieces into every little nook and cranny. Whirtleberry had heard that you can ski in the snow so he packed some wooden ice-cream sticks to strap to their feet so that they could ski as well. Oh, this was so exciting.

The big day arrived, and they hauled their trunk and their little backpacks to their humans' car and clambered in. Everyone in the car was so excited and they sang happy songs as they drove down the highway to the airport. Their favourite song was The Quartermaster's Store, and they sang along with their humans at the tops of their voices. The human dad pulled funny faces and sang in different voices all the time which made everyone laugh.

They arrived at the airport and the humans got a trolley and loaded all of the luggage on top. They placed Whirtleberry and Flapjack at the very, very top of the luggage so that they had a good view. And what a view it was. The airport was so huge and there were so many people. People pushing and squeezing. It was so exciting.

The first trolley that the humans chose had a bad wheel that screeched and squealed all the time: Eeerk, eerk. Wobble, wobble it went. The human dad soon found another trolley and all their bags were moved onto the new trolley.

As they went along Whirtleberry was amazed to see the humans push the trolley onto what looked like a black pavement and as soon as they were on the pavement it whisked them along as fast as anything. They whizzed past other humans who were pushing their trolleys alongside the pavement. When they came to the end of the pavement the humans carried on pushing the trolley.

Whirtleberry thought that this pavement was the most exciting thing he'd seen at the airport. Soon another pavement appeared. Whirtleberry said to Flapjack "I'm going to see what it will be like to scamper along this pavement", and he slipped down to the bottom of the luggage trolley and jumped onto the pavement.

As soon as Whirtleberry's feet touched the pavement he fell over. He could see the trolley with the humans disappearing fast. He got up and started to run on the moving pavement. He was rushing along. He whizzed past people, luggage trolleys and suitcases. Faster and faster he went. He couldn't see his humans and was very worried. He saw the end of the pavement coming and realised that he didn't know how to get off the pavement. How was he to do it? He saw one old man ahead of him who was wearing sandals and socks and as he got to the end of the pavement his socks got caught in the works and he fell over. The pavement sucked his socks off his feet and they disappeared into the machinery. Whirtleberry didn't want to get sucked into the machinery so as he got to the end, he gave a HUGE jump into the air and landed safely away from the grinding machine.

Whirtleberry looked around. Where were his humans. All he could see was feet, shoes, trolleys and suitcases. Oh dear what was he to do. Suddenly he heard shouting coming from the distance. Luckily Flapjack had seen him amongst the crowd, and she was waving and shouting. The humans had stopped pushing the trolley and were looking around so Whirtleberry could get closer. Flapjack took a long scarf out of her luggage and draped it down the side of the trolley. Whirtleberry grabbed hold of it and with Flapjack pulling and Whirtleberry climbing he was soon on the top of the trolley again. He gave Flapjack a big hug and decided he'd had enough adventure for today.

CHAPTER 9

Whirtleberry on the aeroplane

Bing-bing-bong. Bing-bing-bong. There was a loud noise from a loudspeaker and then a voice called out "All passengers on Flight WFH 102 to Seattle board now through Gate five".

There was excited chatter as humans stood up, gathered their bags and started walking towards the boarding gate. Whirtleberry and Flapjack put their little backpacks over their shoulders and followed close behind their humans towards the boarding gate. There were so many legs and shoes and cases that they had to dodge. At the gate, the humans showed their tickets and they started walking towards the plane. Oh, it was so exciting. There was a bridge with glass walls that they crossed that took them to the plane and from the bridge they could see its HUGE engines and WIDE wings.

Soon they were at the entrance. A lady in a uniform took the humans' tickets and then leaned down to look at Whirtleberry and Flapjack and said "Welcome aboard little ones. Enjoy your flight".

Inside the aeroplane were rows and rows of seats. It looked very confusing. But the little mice stayed close to their humans and soon they got to their seats. The humans took all of the bags and put them in the overhead locker. They took Whirtleberry and Flapjack's little bags and put them in the seat pocket in front of them. They sat down and waited while all of the passengers boarded.

Once everyone was aboard the huge doors were closed, CLUNK, and the big engines started revving, Vrooom, swish. Vrooom, swish. Whirtleberry and Flapjack sat on the armrests near the windows and looked out of the windows. The plane started moving down the runway and then with a great noise the engines roared to life and they went speeding down the runway and the next moment they took off into the air and watched the airport, the buildings and the roads with cars on them grow so small below them. Soon all they could see were puffy cotton-wool clouds and the deep blue sea.

After a while the stewardess wheeled a trolley down the aisle. Whirtleberry and Flapjack were very interested to see what she was doing. She was offering drinks and snacks to everyone. She found some teeny-tiny glasses and poured some juice into them and gave them a packet of nuts to nibble on. Oh, they tasted delicious.

On the back of the seats were video screens and the little mice settled down to watch a movie with them. The lights in the cabin were dimmed and soon everyone was asleep.

Whirtleberry opened his eyes. Some people were walking around, and the others had lifted their window blinds and were looking out over the great big fluffy clouds. The early morning sun was shining on the clouds and they looked like big pink candyfloss. Whirtleberry started to feel hungry after seeing the clouds. A stewardess came around with a trolley of warm towels so that they could wipe their faces and she also gave people cups of tea, coffee and fruit juice. Whirtleberry woke up Flapjack and they shared a little cup of steaming hot coffee.

The stewardess came back to them and said that the Captain had heard about them and wondered if they'd like to visit the cockpit where the Captain controlled the plane. Whirtleberry was so excited that he almost fell off the armrest.

The stewardess picked up the little mice and put them onto the trolley and pushed it to the front of the plane. There was a big door in front of her and she knocked and asked if she could come in. The door opened from the inside and she picked up the little mice and put them onto the chair next to the Captain. He lifted them up and put them close to the windscreen so that they could look out at the view.

The clouds had parted and below them they could see the land. There were mountains and sea, lakes and roads. Towns and farmland. It was all so exciting to see. The Captain told the little mice that they would be landing soon and that he needed to make sure that they landed safely. Whirtleberry and Flapjack gave him a tiny hug on his finger and the stewardess took them back to their seats.

Their humans put Whirtleberry and Flapjack back into the seat pockets. They listened to the Vroom Swish, Vroom Swish of the engines again and the plane started getting lower and lower. The houses and cars got closer and closer. Suddenly they were over the airport runway and with a squeak and a rumbling noise they touched down. They had landed and were ready for the next part of their adventure.

CHAPTER 10

Whirtleberry meets Basil

The humans carried Whirtleberry and Flapjack out of the plane and into the airport building. They had to wait at the carousel for their luggage. Whirtleberry and Flapjack loved the carousel and they jumped off the trolley and pulled themselves onto the carousel. Oh, it was such fun as they went round and around. The carousel went behind some thick plastic curtains and the little mice could see the luggage getting unloaded from the plane. Great big crates that were hitched up to carts and got pulled along with a crashing and banging noise.

The little mice came through the thick plastic curtain again and waved to everyone as they rode round and around. Their humans shouted to them to "Be careful! Look out for the luggage!" but the mice were having too much fun to pay much attention.

The next minute an alarm sounded and luggage got thrown onto the carousel. Huge suitcases, bags, boxes and great big bags of golf clubs, push-chairs and even some walking sticks. Whirtleberry shouted to Flapjack, "Look there's our humans' luggage". They scrambled across to the purple and black suitcases and held tight onto the handles. The carousel swung around and soon they could see their humans standing next to the trolley with great big smiles on their faces. The mice scrambled off the luggage and their humans heaved the luggage off the carousel and onto the trolley.

The little mice stood on top of the trolley and looked around. There were so many people and so many doors opening and closing. They got to some big glass doors and there on the other side were more humans. When the doors slid open all the humans started hugging and kissing one another. There was also a dog! Oooh they were scared. He looked so big and fierce. He had a big red floppy tongue that hung to one side and big white teeth. His fur was brown and grey and quite long. Whirtleberry and Flapjack closed their eyes, hugged each other and hid in the luggage.

The little mice suddenly felt hands lifting them up. It was the new humans who gave them a little kiss right on the tippy tip of their noses. It made them sneeze : Aaaah-chooo. "Don't be afraid", said the new human, "This is our dog Basil and he's been longing to meet you. He's so excited to have some new friends". The human held them out on the palms of her hands and lowered them towards the dog, Basil. Basil leaned forward and sniffed at the little mice, then he gave them a big slobbery, wet kiss to welcome them. Basil had on a backpack where there were two little pockets just the right size for Whirtleberry and Flapjack. He walked along with them on his back while the humans walked behind pushing the trolley until they reached the car.

All of the luggage was put into the back of the car and soon they set off. Whirtleberry and Flapjack sat at the back with Basil. They could look out of the windows at all the new sights. There were different cars to home and they drove on the opposite side of the road. The trees and houses looked different and, what was this, there was white stuff all over the ground. It was snow. This was the snow that they'd been talking about at home. Whirtleberry and Flapjack were so excited. They could not wait to get to the house and explore the snow.

Soon they were home and they rushed inside with their luggage. Basil was barking with excitement. He wanted to show them all about the snow. They got into warm coats, mittens and warm boots and went outside with the humans. Basil raced ahead and jumped into a snowdrift where he disappeared into the snow. He burst out of the snow and came racing back to the mice.

Whirtleberry and Flapjack stepped cautiously into the snow. They also disappeared. Their humans reached down and picked them up and put little mice sized snowshoes onto them so that they wouldn't disappear again. They stomped around on top of the snow and made little snowballs that they threw at each other, giggling all the time. Basil raced back to them and barked and tried to catch the snowballs that they were throwing. Everyone was having so much fun.

The mice started to get a bit cold and tired, so they all went inside to the warm lounge where a fire was burning in the fireplace. The humans made hot chocolate for everyone which they sipped in front of the fire. The little mice soon grew drowsy and their little eyes closed, and they fell fast asleep cuddled up with Basil.

THE END

Printed in the United States
by Baker & Taylor Publisher Services